Dd dance

Ee

Ff

Jj

Kk kangaroo

Ll

Oo

pail

Pp

Qq

umbrella

Uu

vegetables

Vv

Yy

Zz

zebra

My First Muppet Dictionary

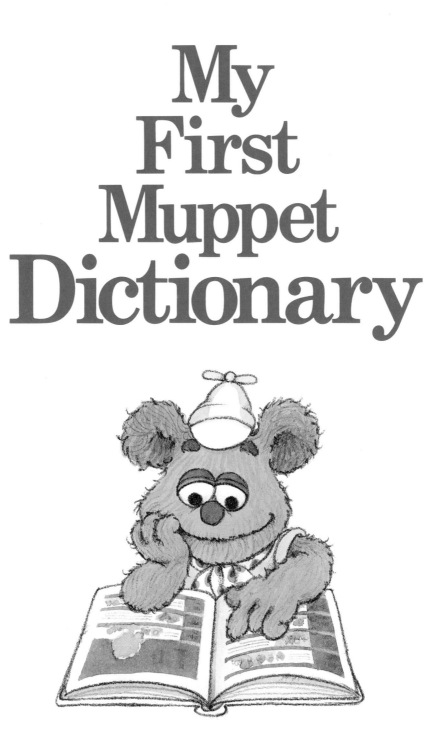

Edited by Louise Gikow, Justine Korman, and Rita Rosenkranz

Designed by Sandra Forrest
Illustrated by Tom Cooke

Bendon Publishing International

Special thanks to Lauren Attinello, Barbara Brenner,
Didi Charney, and Rick Pracher for their invaluable assistance,
and to Bruce McNally for his design concept.

A Letter from Jim Henson

One of the most important things we can do for our children is to encourage them to enjoy reading. I am therefore particularly delighted to introduce to you **My First Muppet Dictionary.**

This dictionary was designed to encourage young children to take an active interest in the words they speak and read. The language of the dictionary is simple and clear, and a special effort was made to define all the words in ways that children can easily understand. In addition, many of the words are woven into little illustrated "stories," making the dictionary fun to open at any point and just read.

Most of all, **My First Muppet Dictionary** was created in the hope that parents would look at it and read it *with* their children. If you encourage them to use a dictionary as they are learning to read, your children may well continue to do so as they grow up. This can improve their reading skills, strengthen their writing, and give them a strong appreciation of the English language.

I hope both you and your children will enjoy **My First Muppet Dictionary.**

Jim Henson

How to Use This Dictionary

Hi! This is Baby Kermit. Welcome to **My First Muppet Dictionary**! I'm here to tell you a little bit about how to use this book. It's really very easy.

To find a word, the first thing you have to do is figure out what the first letter of the word is. (Grown-ups can be very helpful with this.) Once you know, find the section for that letter of the alphabet. For instance, the word below is **pail,** so to find it, you'd have to find the section for **P.**

Now, suppose you wanted to know the meaning of the word **pail.** Follow me, and I'll show you what to look for!

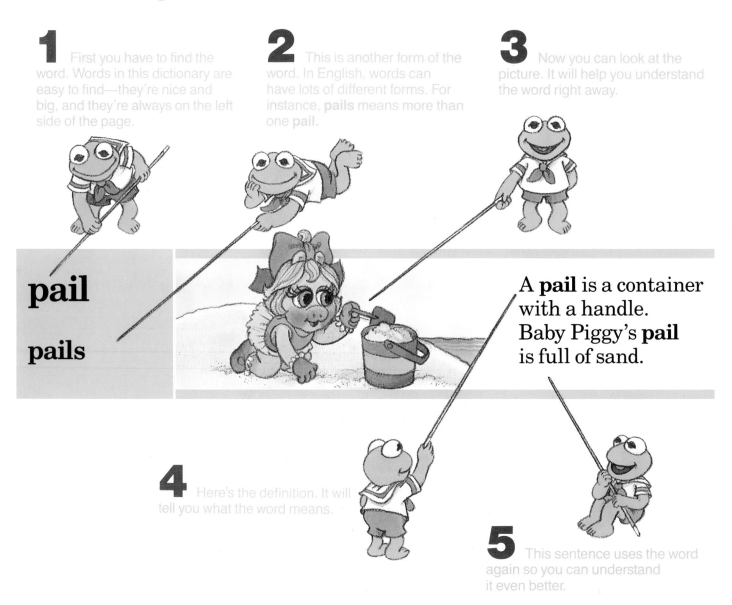

1 First you have to find the word. Words in this dictionary are easy to find—they're nice and big, and they're always on the left side of the page.

2 This is another form of the word. In English, words can have lots of different forms. For instance, **pails** means more than one **pail.**

3 Now you can look at the picture. It will help you understand the word right away.

pail

pails

A **pail** is a container with a handle. Baby Piggy's **pail** is full of sand.

4 Here's the definition. It will tell you what the word means.

5 This sentence uses the word again so you can understand it even better.

See? I told you it was easy!

There's something else that's neat about this dictionary. Some of the pictures tell little stories or ask you questions. If you want to see what I mean, look at **whale** and **what.**

whale

whales

A **whale** is a big animal that lives in the ocean. Pirate Kermit sees **whales** from his boat.

what

What is a word that often asks a question. **What** is that big animal swimming in the water?

And just one more thing: Look at the definition under **whale** again. Do you want to know what the word **ocean** means? Well, just look it up under **O.** We've tried really hard to define most of the words that are in this book. (But if we've missed a few, just ask a grown-up to help.)

Well, I think I'm going to read a book myself right now. Have fun with the dictionary!

A Note to Grown-ups

This dictionary was carefully researched to include as many early vocabulary words as possible. We also attempted to include all the major definitions of words for children, so there sometimes are two definitions per word. But no dictionary says it all—and that's where *you* come in. We highly recommend using this dictionary with your child. You can help define additional words, and you can also point out to them those words that have more than one meaning in English. Learning about language can be a wonderful game—and you and your child can have a lot of fun using **My First Muppet Dictionary,** especially if you use it together.

A a

above

Above means over or higher than. There is a clock **above** Baby Kermit's head.

after

After is the opposite of before. Baby Piggy and Baby Kermit clean up **after** breakfast.

air

Air is what we breathe. **Air** is all around us.

airplane

airplanes

An **airplane** is a machine that flies. Baby Skeeter wants to fly an **airplane** when she grows up.

all

All means the whole of something.
Baby Animal has **all** the apples.

angry

Angry is being mad about something.
Baby Animal is **angry** because his
toy airplane is broken.

animal

animals

An **animal** is a living
thing that is not a plant.
An ape is an **animal**.

ankle

ankles

Your **ankle** joins your foot to your leg.
Simon says: Grab your **ankle**.

ant

ants

An **ant** is an insect.
An **ant** is not an aunt.
This **ant** lives in that anthill.

ape

apes

An **ape** is a smart animal that
looks like a big monkey.
Apes can walk on
two legs.
This **ape** is asleep.

apple
apples

An **apple** is a round fruit
that grows on trees.
Baby Animal has lots of **apples**.

arm
arms

Your **arm** is between your
shoulder and your wrist.
Simon says: Raise your **arms**.

ask
asks

You **ask** a question when you
want to know something.
Baby Kermit **asks** Animal how
many apples he has.

asleep

When people and animals are
not awake, they are **asleep**.
Baby Gonzo dreams when
he is **asleep**.

aunt
aunts

Your **aunt** is the sister of
your father or mother.
Your **aunts** and uncles
are part of your family.

awake

When people and animals are
not asleep, they are **awake**.
Baby Gonzo is asleep, but
Baby Animal is wide **awake**.

Bb

baby

babies

A **baby** is a very young person or animal. Animal is still a **baby**. He can't walk yet.

back

Back is the opposite of front. Your **back** is also a part of your body. Baby Gonzo is scratching his **back**.

bad

Bad is the opposite of good. It is **bad** to write on the walls.

bake

bakes

To **bake** is to cook something in an oven. The Swedish Chef **bakes** bread.

ball

balls

A **ball** is a round toy or thing.
Baby Piggy plays with the **ball**.

barn

barns

A **barn** is a house for
animals on a farm.
Baby Gonzo takes the
cow to the **barn**.

bath

baths

A **bath** is lots of water and
soap to clean your body.
Baby Kermit takes a **bath**
with his boat.

beach

beaches

A **beach** is the sand by
an ocean or lake.
Baby Kermit and Baby Piggy
play ball at the **beach**.

bean

beans

A **bean** is a vegetable.
Beans can be green, yellow,
red, white, or black.

bear

bears

A **bear** is a furry wild animal.
This **bear** loves to eat honey.

bed

beds

A **bed** is something soft to sleep in.
Baby Gonzo puts Camilla into her **bed**.

bee

bees

A **bee** is a small insect.
Some **bees** make honey.

before

Before is the opposite of after.
Baby Animal brushes his teeth **before** going to bed.

bell

bells

A **bell** is for ringing.
Baby Fozzie rings the dinner **bell**.

below

Below is the opposite of above.
There is a bee **below** the bell.

big

Big means large, not small.
This bear is so **big**, we can only see his feet.

bird
birds

A **bird** is an animal with feathers and wings. This **bird** is feeding her babies.

birthday
birthdays

Your **birthday** is the day you were born. People often have parties on their **birthdays**.

black

Black is the darkest color. The big **black** bear sits in a blue boat.

blanket
blankets

Your **blanket** covers you in bed. Baby Rowlf pulls up his **blanket**.

blue

Blue is a color. Baby Gonzo flies his **blue** airplane in the **blue** sky over the **blue** lake.

boat
boats

You travel on water in a **boat**. Baby Kermit rows the **boat**.

body

bodies

A **body** is all the parts of something, including you. Can you name all the parts of your **body**?

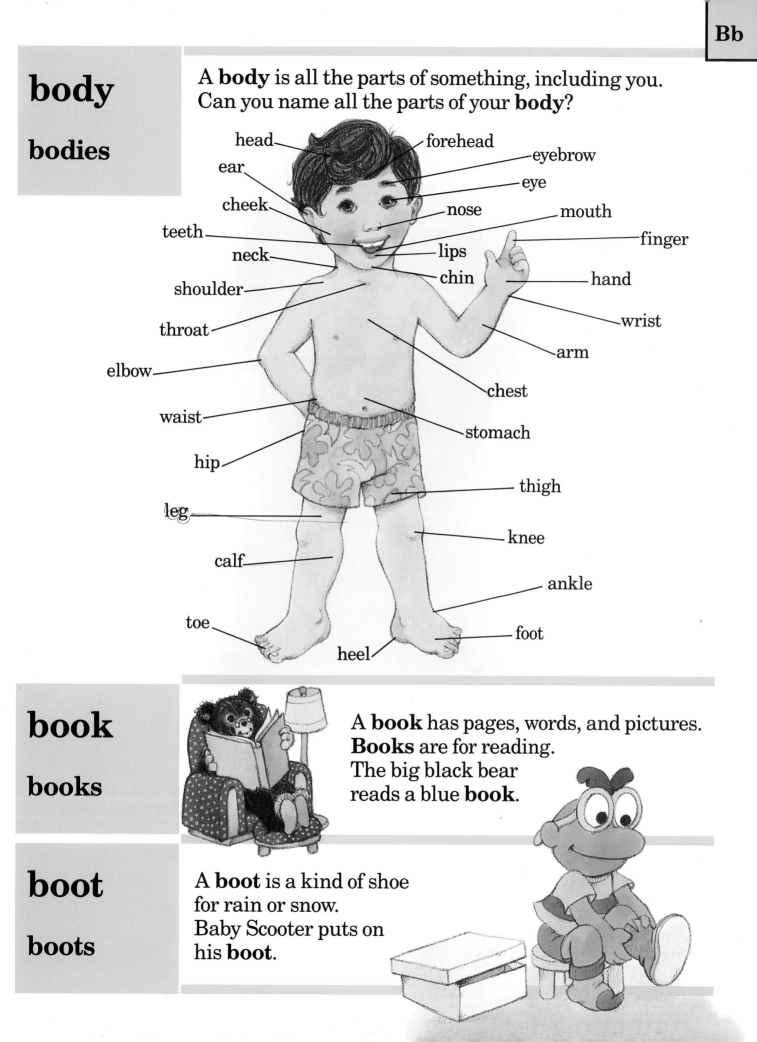

head — forehead — eyebrow — eye — ear — cheek — nose — mouth — teeth — finger — neck — lips — chin — hand — shoulder — wrist — throat — arm — elbow — chest — waist — stomach — hip — thigh — leg — knee — calf — ankle — toe — foot — heel

book

books

A **book** has pages, words, and pictures. **Books** are for reading. The big black bear reads a blue **book**.

boot

boots

A **boot** is a kind of shoe for rain or snow. Baby Scooter puts on his **boot**.

bottle

bottles

A **bottle** is a container that can hold liquids. Baby Kermit pours milk from a **bottle**.

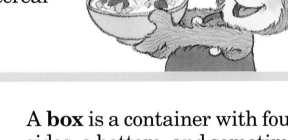

bowl

bowls

A **bowl** is a round dish. Baby Gonzo has cereal in his **bowl**.

box

boxes

A **box** is a container with four sides, a bottom, and sometimes a lid. Baby Scooter's other boot is in the **box**.

boy

boys

A **boy** is a male child. The **boy** throws the ball to the dog.

bread

Bread is a food made with flour and baked in an oven. Baby Piggy puts butter on her **bread**.

breakfast

breakfasts

You eat **breakfast** in the morning. The Muppet Babies are eating **breakfast**.

brother
brothers

Your **brother** is a boy who has the same mother and father as you do. Scooter is Skeeter's **brother**.

brown

Brown is the color of chocolate. Baby Rowlf is **brown**.

brush
brushes

You use a **brush** to keep your hair neat, clean your teeth, or paint. Baby Piggy brushes her hair with a **brush**.

butter

Butter is a yellow food that is made from milk. Baby Fozzie puts **butter** on his corn.

butterfly
butterflies

A **butterfly** is an insect with colorful wings. Three yellow **butterflies** fly in the air.

button
buttons

You keep your clothes closed with **buttons**. Baby Gonzo buttons one **button** at a time.

C c

cake

cakes

Cake is a sweet, baked dessert. Baby Kermit's birthday **cake** has four candles on it.

car

cars

A **car** has four wheels and an engine. You go places in a **car**. Baby Kermit got a toy **car** for his birthday.

carrot

carrots

A **carrot** is an orange vegetable. **Carrots** grow in the ground.

cat

cats

A **cat** is a small, furry animal that makes a good pet. The **cat** plays with a ball.

catch

catches

To **catch** is to get or grab. Baby Fozzie **catches** the ball.

cave

caves

A **cave** is a big hole in rock or earth. This **cave** is very dark.

chair

chairs

A **chair** is furniture to sit on. Baby Bunsen sits on a **chair**.

cheese

cheeses

Cheese is a food made from milk. The mouse eats the **cheese**.

chest

chests

A **chest** is a box to keep things in. Also, your **chest** is between your neck and your stomach. Baby Animal wears a bib that covers his **chest**.

chew

chews

You **chew** with your teeth. Baby Animal **chews** on an apple.

chicken

chickens

A **chicken** is a kind of bird. This **chicken** lives on a farm.

child

children

A **child** is a boy or girl. The **child** helps Statler cross the street.

chin

chins

Your **chin** is the part of your face below your mouth. Baby Bunsen has chocolate ice cream all over his **chin**.

chocolate

chocolates

Chocolate is a sweet food. Baby Bunsen likes **chocolate** ice cream.

circle

circles

A **circle** is a round and flat shape. Baby Rowlf draws a **circle**.

city

cities

A **city** is bigger than a town. Many people live in a **city**.

clap

claps

To **clap** is to hit your hands together to make a sound. The Muppet Babies **clap** their hands.

clay

You use **clay** to make things. Baby Gonzo makes a chicken from **clay**.

clean

cleans

To **clean** is to tidy up or wash away dirt. The Muppet Babies **clean** the window.

climb

climbs

To **climb** is to go up. Baby Kermit **climbs** up the ladder.

clock

clocks

A **clock** is an instrument that tells time. Baby Rowlf fixes the **clock**.

clothes

Clothes are what you wear on your body. Shirts and skirts are **clothes**.

cloud

clouds

A **cloud** is many small drops of water floating together in the sky. Rain comes from **clouds**.

clown

clowns

Clowns are people who make you laugh. Baby Fozzie pretends to be a **clown**.

coat

coats

A **coat** is something to wear when it is rainy or cold. Baby Rowlf wears his new **coat**.

cold

Cold is the opposite of hot. Kermit and Rowlf like to play outside when it is **cold**.

color

colors

Baby Gonzo is using many **colors** in his picture.

red orange yellow green blue purple violet

comb

combs

A **comb** has long, thin teeth.
You use a **comb** to keep your
hair neat.
Baby Piggy combs her doll's
hair with a **comb**.

come

comes

To **come** is to move toward
someone or something.

Please **come** to the table,
Baby Animal.

cook

cooks

To **cook** is to prepare
food by heating it.
The Swedish Chef
cooks soup in a pot.

cookie

cookies

A **cookie** is a small, flat cake.
Baby Gonzo saves his
cookie for dessert.

corn

Corn is a vegetable that
people and animals eat.
Baby Piggy likes
to eat **corn**.

count

counts

You **count** to find out how many
things there are.
How many cookies can you **count**
on this page? (Answer below.)

Answer: There are eight cookies on this page. Did you **count** the cookie near the cookie definition?

cover

covers

To **cover** is to put one thing over something else. Baby Gonzo **covers** himself with his blanket.

cow

cows

A **cow** is a big animal. Milk comes from **cows.** This **cow** is brown.

crawl

crawls

To **crawl** is to move on hands and knees. Baby Animal **crawls** on the floor.

cry

cries

To **cry** is to sob or weep when you're sad or hurt. Why does Baby Animal **cry?**

cup

cups

A **cup** is a small bowl with a handle. Baby Animal has spilled his **cup** of milk.

cut

cuts

To **cut** is to make pieces out of something. Baby Piggy **cuts** a circle out of paper.

D d

dad
dads

Dad is another word for father.
This **dad** and his daughter are ice-skating.

dance
dances

To **dance** is to move to music.
Baby Piggy loves to **dance** all day.

dark

Dark is when there is little or no light.
Baby Piggy goes to bed when it is **dark**.

daughter
daughters

If you are a girl, you are the **daughter** of your mother and father.
Two **daughters** of the same mother and father are sisters.

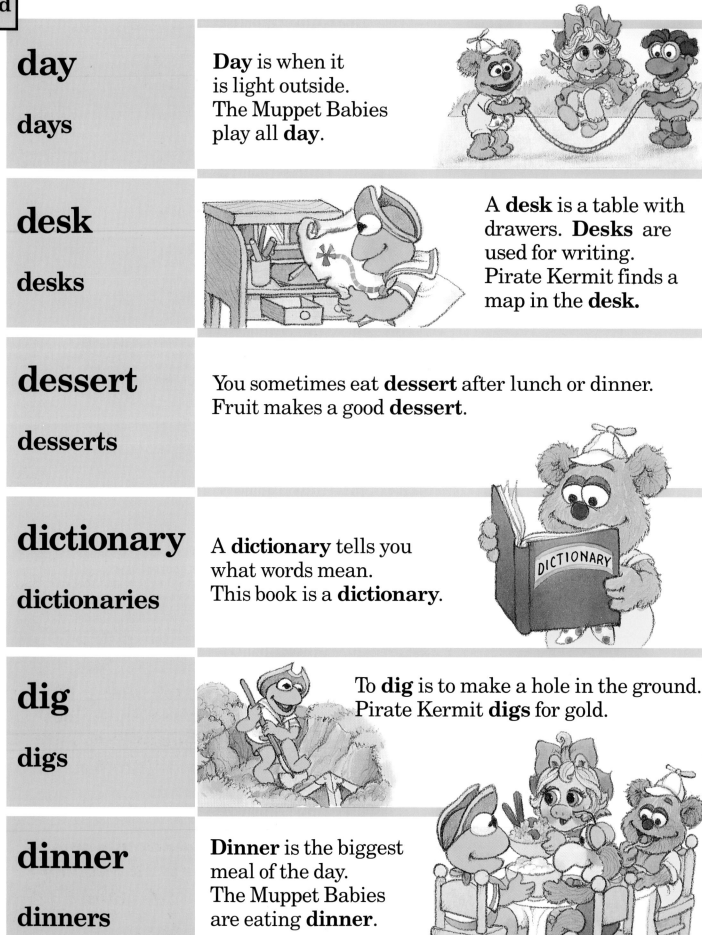

day

days

Day is when it is light outside. The Muppet Babies play all **day**.

desk

desks

A **desk** is a table with drawers. **Desks** are used for writing. Pirate Kermit finds a map in the **desk.**

dessert

desserts

You sometimes eat **dessert** after lunch or dinner. Fruit makes a good **dessert**.

dictionary

dictionaries

A **dictionary** tells you what words mean. This book is a **dictionary**.

dig

digs

To **dig** is to make a hole in the ground. Pirate Kermit **digs** for gold.

dinner

dinners

Dinner is the biggest meal of the day. The Muppet Babies are eating **dinner**.

dirt

Dirt is mud or earth. Baby Animal is covered with **dirt**.

dish

dishes

A **dish** is a plate that holds food. Baby Piggy carries a **dish**.

dive

dives

To **dive** is to jump headfirst into something, usually water. Baby Gonzo **dives** into the pool.

do

does

When you make something happen, you **do** it. Baby Gonzo **does** a fantastic double flip.

doctor

doctors

A **doctor** takes care of you when you get sick. The **doctor** looks in Baby Piggy's ear.

dog

dogs

A **dog** is a furry animal that barks. Some **dogs** are big; other **dogs** are small.

doll

dolls

A **doll** is a toy that looks like a baby, a child, a man, or a woman.

Baby Piggy's **doll** wears a green dress.

door

doors

A **door** is an opening for going in or out. The **door** is open.

down

To go **down** is to move from a higher place to a lower place. Baby Gonzo goes **down** the stairs.

draw

draws

To **draw** is to make a picture or shape. Baby Gonzo **draws** a picture of Baby Piggy's doll.

drawer

drawers

A **drawer** is a place to keep things. Baby Piggy finds her comb in the **drawer**.

dream

dreams

A **dream** is something you see while you sleep. In Baby Skeeter's **dream**, she flies an airplane.

dress

dresses

Dresses are clothes that women and girls wear. Baby Piggy wears a pink **dress**.

drink

drinks

To **drink** is to swallow liquid. Baby Fozzie **drinks** his milk.

drive

drives

To **drive** is to make something go. Baby Kermit **drives** his car to the store.

drum

drums

A **drum** is an instrument that you hit to make a sound. Baby Animal plays a big **drum**.

dry

Dry is the opposite of wet. To stay **dry**, use an umbrella.

duck

ducks

A **duck** is a web-footed bird that swims. The **duck** likes to get wet.

E e

ear

ears

You hear sounds with your **ears**. Baby Fozzie scratches his **ear**.

early

You are **early** when you do something before most other people do it. Farmers work **early** in the morning.

earth

Earth is ground or dirt. **Earth** is also the planet we live on. Baby Gonzo goes from **earth** to the moon.

easy

Easy means not hard to do. Flying a rocket is **easy** for Baby Gonzo.

eat
eats

To **eat** is to chew and swallow food. Baby Animal wants to **eat** everything.

egg
eggs

An **egg** can be food. Some baby birds or other animals hatch from **eggs**.
The chicken has an **egg** in her nest.

eight

Eight is the number after seven and before nine. A spider has **eight** legs.

elbow
elbows

Your **elbow** is where your arm bends. Baby Piggy wears bracelets up to her **elbow**.

elephant
elephants

An **elephant** is a very big animal. The **elephant** has a long nose called a trunk.

end
ends

The **end** is the last part of something. This is the **end** of this page.

engine
engines

An **engine** makes things go.
A car has an **engine**.

erase
erases

To **erase** is to remove.
Baby Gonzo **erases**
his drawing.

explore
explores

To **explore** is to search
or examine.
Baby Kermit **explores**
the cave.

extra

Something you don't need is **extra**.
Baby Piggy has one **extra** sock.

eye
eyes

You look and see
with your **eyes**.
Baby Fozzie is
rubbing his **eye**.

eyebrow
eyebrows

Your **eyebrow** is the line
of hair that grows
above your eye.
Baby Fozzie raises
his **eyebrows**.

F f

face

faces

Eyes, nose, cheeks, forehead, mouth, and chin make a **face**. Baby Piggy looks at her **face** in the mirror.

fall

falls

Fall is the season between summer and winter.
Also, to **fall** is to drop down from a higher place.
The apple **falls** off the tree.

family

families

A **family** is made up of related people, animals, or things.
Some **families** are big; other **families** are small.

far

Far is the opposite of near.
Gonzo is **far** away.

farm
farms

A **farm** is a place where people grow plants and raise animals. Baby Gonzo visits the chickens on the **farm**.

fast

Fast means at great speed. It is the opposite of slow. Baby Kermit runs very **fast**.

fat

Fat is the opposite of thin. The **fat** cat ate the cake.

father
fathers

A **father** is a man who has a child. This girl's **father** is a farmer.

feel
feels

To **feel** is to touch something with your hand. Also, you can **feel** happy or sad. Baby Fozzie **feels** happy.

find
finds

To **find** is to discover. Can you **find** the fox in this picture?

finger

fingers

Your **finger** is part of your hand.
How many **fingers** is
Baby Kermit holding up?

fire

Fire is heat and light caused
when something burns.
Statler sits in front of the **fire**.

first

First comes before
anything else.
Baby Piggy is **first**
in line for breakfast.

fish

A **fish** is an animal
that lives in water.
Fish use their fins
to move about.

five

Five is the number after
four and before six.
There are **five** fish
in the fishbowl.

fix

fixes

To **fix** is to make something work
that has been broken.
Baby Animal **fixes** his toy
airplane with glue.

Glue

float

floats

To **float** is to rest on the water.
Baby Kermit **floats** on the lake.

floor

floors

The **floor** is what you
walk on inside.
Baby Scooter plays
on the **floor**.

flour

Flour is used to make some foods.
Bread, cake, and noodles
are made from **flour**.

flower

flowers

A **flower** is a plant.
Flowers come in all colors.
Baby Kermit gives
Baby Piggy a **flower**.

fly

flies

To **fly** is to move through the
air like a bird.
Baby Skeeter **flies** in an airplane.

fold

folds

To **fold** is to bend part of
something over the rest of it.
Baby Rowlf **folds** a piece of paper
to make a paper airplane.

food

foods

People, animals, and plants need **food** to live.
Baby Piggy eats a lot of **food**.

foot

feet

At the end of your leg is your **foot**.
Baby Fozzie holds his **foot**.

fork

forks

A **fork** is a tool for picking up things like food.
Baby Piggy eats with a **fork**.

four

Four is the number after three and before five.
This monster has **four** feet, **four** legs, **four** arms, and **four** eyes.

fox

foxes

A **fox** is a wild animal in the dog family.
Is this **fox** in Baby Rowlf's family?

friend

friends

Friends are people whom you like and who also like you.
Baby Fozzie is Kermit's **friend**.

frog
frogs

A **frog** is a small animal that lives both on the ground and in the water. The **frog** hops into the water.

front

Front is the opposite of back. Baby Piggy is at the **front** of the line.

fruit
fruits

Fruit is a sweet food that grows on trees and bushes. There are three kinds of **fruit** in this bowl: apples, grapes, and peaches.

fun

Fun is having a good time. The Muppet Babies are having **fun**.

fur

Fur is the soft hair that covers some animals. Baby Fozzie has **fur**.

Gg

game

games

A **game** is something you play. Leapfrog is a **game**.

gift

gifts

A **gift** is something you give to someone. Baby Kermit gives Piggy a birthday **gift**.

giraffe

giraffes

A **giraffe** is an animal with a long neck. The **giraffe** eats leaves for dinner.

girl

girls

A **girl** is a female child. The **girl** feeds the giraffe.

give
gives

Give is the opposite of take. Gonzo **gives** Camilla some grapes.

glass
glasses

A **glass** is something you drink from. Also, **glass** is hard, clear, and easy to break. Windows are usually made of **glass**.

glove
gloves

A **glove** is a mitten with a place for each finger. Baby Piggy pulls on her **gloves**.

glue

Glue is a liquid used to stick things together. Baby Gonzo uses **glue** to make his toy rocket.

go
goes

To **go** is to move from one place to another place. The car **goes** up the hill.

goat
goats

A **goat** is an animal with four legs and two horns. **Goats** like to climb hills.

gold

Gold is a yellow metal.
Baby Piggy likes this **gold** ring.

good

Good is the opposite of bad.
Baby Animal is doing a
good job of putting
away his toys.

good-bye

Good-bye is the opposite
of hello.
Baby Kermit waves
good-bye to Baby Fozzie.

grandfather

grandfathers

Your **grandfather** is the father
of your mother or father.
The boy visits his
grandfather and grandmother.

grandmother

grandmothers

Your **grandmother** is the mother
of your father or mother.
The boy's **grandmother**
and grandfather are
happy to see him.

grape

grapes

A **grape** is a fruit that grows in bunches.
Grapes are used to make juice and jelly.

grass

gray

green

ground

grow

grows

guess

guesses

Grass is a green plant that grows in the ground.
Grass grows in the park.

Gray is the color
you get when you
mix black and white.
This rabbit is gray.

Green is the color of grass.
Kermit is happy
to be green.

The ground is
the earth.
The flowers grow
in the ground.

To grow is to get bigger.
Water and sun help
flowers to grow.

When you don't know the answer
to a question, you guess.
Guess which hand holds the grapes?

H h

hair
hairs

Hair covers parts of your head and other parts of your body. Beaker has red **hair**.

hammer
hammers

A **hammer** is a tool. The man hammers the nail with a **hammer**.

hand
hands

Your **hands** are at the ends of your wrists. Baby Fozzie waves his **hand**.

handle
handles

You hold something by its **handle**. Baby Animal picks up the cup by its **handle**.

happy

When you are **happy**, you feel good. Baby Piggy is **happy** that Kermit is giving her a gift.

hard

Hard is the opposite of soft. **Hard** is also the opposite of easy. It is **hard** for Baby Animal to tie his shoelaces.

hat

hats

A **hat** covers your head. The horse wears a **hat**.

head

heads

Your **head** is a part of your body. **Head** also means the top of something.

hear

hears

People and animals **hear** sounds with their ears. The horse **hears** the horn.

heart

hearts

The **heart** is a muscle that helps move blood through the body. A **heart** is also a shape.

Hello.

hello

Hello is what you say when you meet someone. Baby Fozzie says **hello** to Baby Kermit.

help

helps

You **help** people or animals when they need you. Baby Kermit **helps** Piggy dig a hole.

hide

hides

To **hide** is to disappear so that no one can find you. One goat **hides** behind a tree.

high

High is the opposite of low. Baby Fozzie is **high** up on the hill.

hill

hills

A **hill** is a mound of earth or sand or rock. There are goats on the **hill**.

hip

hips

Your **hip** is below your waist and above your leg. Simon says: Put your hands on your **hips**.

hit

hits

To **hit** is to strike something with your hand or with something else. Baby Kermit **hits** the ball.

hold

holds

To **hold** is to carry or grasp. Baby Kermit **holds** the bat.

hole

holes

A **hole** is an opening or a space in something. There is a **hole** in the tree.

honey

Honey is a sweet food that bees make. Baby Piggy puts some **honey** in her basket.

hood

hoods

A **hood** covers your head and neck. What color is Baby Piggy's **hood**?

hop

hops

To **hop** is to jump up and down on one foot or both feet. The rabbit **hops** across the road.

horn

horns

A **horn** is an instrument that you blow into to make a sound. **Horns** also grow on some animals' heads.

horse

horses

A **horse** is an animal with four legs. Cowboy Kermit rides a **horse**.

hot

Hot is the opposite of cold. Fire is too **hot** to touch.

hour

hours

One **hour** is sixty minutes. There are twenty-four **hours** in a day.

house

houses

A **house** is a building that people live in. Why is the horse in the **house**?

hurt

hurts

To **hurt** is to make someone or yourself feel bad. Skeeter **hurt** her knee.

I i

I am Baby Kermit.

I

I is a word you use when you talk about yourself.

ice

Ice is frozen water. Baby Bunsen ice-skates across the **ice**.

ice cream

Ice cream is a food made from milk. Baby Piggy eats **ice cream**.

idea

ideas

An **idea** is something you think of. Baby Bunsen has a good **idea**! He is using an umbrella to move faster.

in

In is the opposite of out.
The teddy bear is **in** the box.

ink

Ink is a colored liquid
that you use to write
or draw.
Kermit loves to draw
in green **ink**.

insect

insects

An **insect** is a tiny
animal with six legs.
Some **insects** fly;
other **insects** crawl.

inside

Inside means to be
in something.
Baby Kermit is **inside**
the house.

iron

irons

An **iron** is something
used to press clothes.
Iron is also a metal.

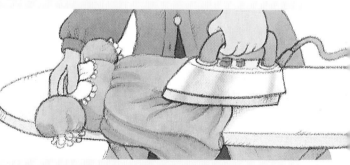

itch

itches

An **itch** is a feeling that makes
you want to scratch.
An insect bite often **itches**.

Jj

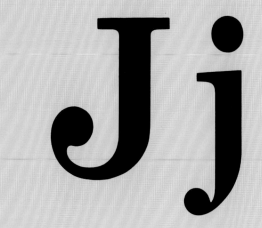

jacket

jackets

A **jacket** is something you wear to keep warm. Baby Kermit has a new red winter **jacket**.

jar

jars

A **jar** is a container for food or other things. Baby Animal puts the lid on the **jar** of jelly.

jelly

jellies

Jelly is a sweet food made from fruit. Baby Animal makes a peanut butter-and-**jelly** sandwich.

jet

jets

A **jet** is a kind of airplane. The **jet** flies over the ocean.

job
jobs

A **job** is work that you do. Baby Kermit's **job** is to shovel the snow.

join
joins

To **join** is to put two or more things together. Baby Fozzie **joins** his friends.

joke
jokes

A **joke** makes you laugh. Baby Fozzie tells a **joke** to Baby Kermit and Baby Piggy.

juice

Juice is a liquid made by squeezing fruits or vegetables. Baby Animal drinks orange **juice**.

jump
jumps

To **jump** is to lift your feet off the ground at the same time. The cow **jumps** over the moon.

jungle
jungles

A **jungle** is a wild place with plants and animals. Baby Kermit drives through the **jungle**.

K k

kangaroo

kangaroos

A **kangaroo** is a big animal that carries its babies in a pouch on its stomach. The **kangaroo** hops on two strong legs.

keep

keeps

To **keep** is to have something for a long time. Baby Kermit **keeps** the key.

key

keys

A **key** opens or closes a lock. Baby Kermit uses the **key** to unlock the door.

kick

kicks

To **kick** is to hit with your foot. Baby Fozzie **kicks** the ball.

Kk

kind

To be **kind** is to be nice. The king is **kind** to the knight.

king

kings

A **king** is a man who is the leader of a country. The **king** wears a gold crown.

kiss

kisses

To **kiss** is to touch with the lips. Baby Piggy **kisses** Baby Kermit.

kitchen

kitchens

A **kitchen** is a room where people cook food. The Swedish Chef cooks corn in the **kitchen**.

kite

kites

A **kite** is a toy with a long string. **Kites** fly in the wind. Baby Gonzo flies his **kite** at the beach.

kitten

kittens

A **kitten** is a baby cat. The **kitten** plays with the string on Baby Gonzo's kite.

learn

learns

When you **learn** something, you know it. Baby Fozzie **learns** to read.

left

Left is the opposite of right. The ball is on the **left**.

leg

legs

Your **leg** is between your hip and your foot. Simon says: Shake your **leg**!

letter

letters

A **letter** is part of a word. A **letter** is also something you write to someone.

lift

lifts

To **lift** is to pick something up. Baby Kermit **lifts** the apples.

light

Light is the opposite of dark. It is **light** during the day.

like

likes

To **like** is to enjoy someone or something. Baby Kermit **likes** Piggy. He also **likes** apples.

line

lines

A **line** is a long, thin mark. Baby Rowlf writes a letter between the **lines**.

lion

lions

A **lion** is a big, wild animal. You can see **lions** at the zoo.

lip

lips

Lips are the two parts of your face around your mouth. You use your **lips** to smile, talk, and kiss.

liquid

liquids

A **liquid** is wet. Milk and water are **liquids**.

long

Long is the opposite of short. The giraffes have **long** necks.

look

looks

To **look** is to use your eyes to see something. Baby Kermit helps Baby Piggy **look** for her mittens.

lose

loses

If you **lose** something, you can't find it. It is easy to **lose** white mittens in the snow.

loud

Loud is the opposite of quiet or soft. Baby Animal makes a **loud** sound on his drum.

love

loves

To **love** is to like very much. Baby Fozzie **loves** his teddy bear.

low

Low is the opposite of high. Baby Animal's chair is too **low**.

lunch

lunches

You eat **lunch** in the middle of the day. Baby Gonzo eats a pickle-and-cheese sandwich for **lunch**.

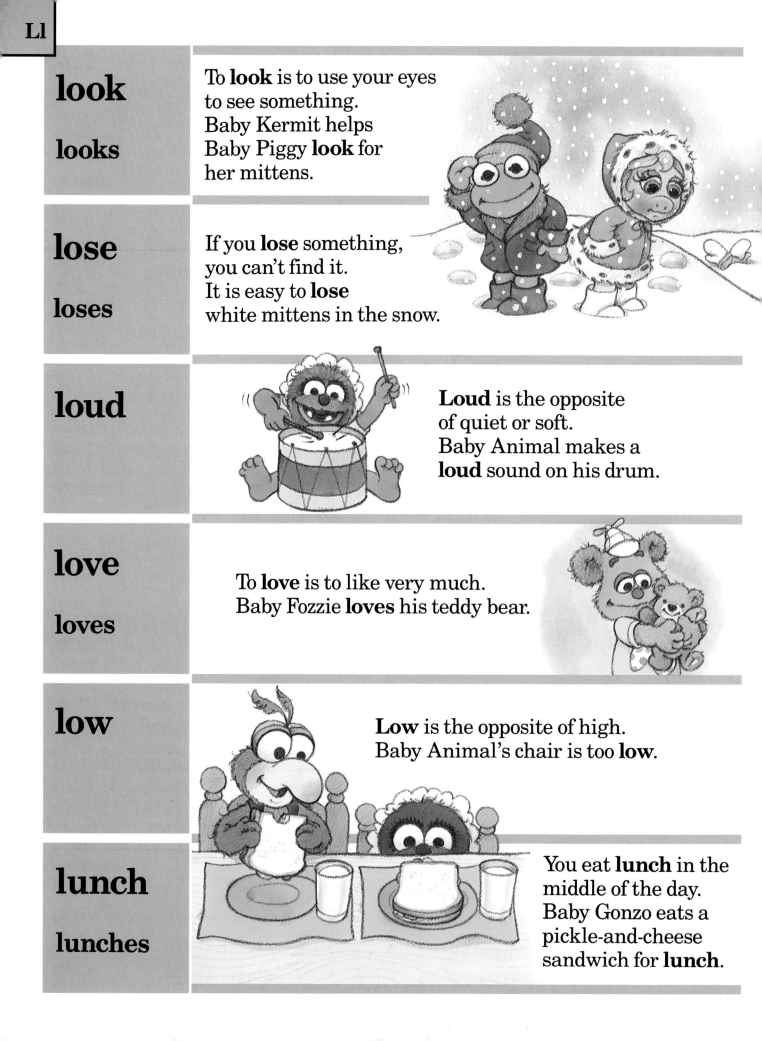

Mm

mad

When you are **mad**, you are angry.
Baby Piggy is **mad** that there are no more apples.

make

makes

When you **make** a thing, you have something that wasn't there before.
Baby Gonzo **makes** a mask from paper.

man

men

When a boy grows up, he is a **man**.
This **man** has a son and a daughter.

map

maps

A **map** is a picture that shows where something is.
Pirate Kermit's **map** shows where the treasure is.

mask
masks

A **mask** covers your face.
Baby Gonzo wears a **mask**
on Halloween.

me

Me is a word you use when
you talk about yourself.

I'll bet you didn't know
me with my mask on!

metal
metals

Metal is a hard material
used to make things like cars,
airplanes, and tools.
This pot is made of **metal**.

milk

Milk is a white liquid that
many people and animals drink.
The **milk** we drink usually
comes from cows.

minute
minutes

One **minute** is sixty seconds.
There are sixty **minutes** in an hour.

mitten
mittens

A **mitten** covers your hand
and keeps it warm.
Baby Piggy wears **mittens**
when it's cold.

mix

mixes

To **mix** is to stir together. Baby Kermit **mixes** milk, eggs, and flour to make pancakes.

mom

moms

Mom is another word for mother. The child waves to her **mom**.

monkey

monkeys

A **monkey** is an animal with long arms and legs. **Monkeys** like to climb trees.

month

months

One **month** is about four weeks. There are twelve **months** in a year: January, February, March, April, May, June, July, August, September, October, November, and December.

moon

moons

The **moon** is an object that travels around the earth. We often see the **moon** in the sky at night.

morning

mornings

The **morning** is the first part of the day. Baby Kermit wakes up in the **morning**.

mother

mothers

A **mother** is a woman who has a child.
Other words for **mother** are mom and mommy.

mouse

mice

Mice are small animals with long tails. This **mouse** lives in a mouse hole.

mouth

mouths

Your **mouth** is the part of your face that you eat and talk with. Don't talk with your **mouth** full!

move

moves

To **move** is to not stand still. People can also **move** to another house.

mud

When you mix dirt and water, you get **mud**. Baby Animal likes to make **mud** pies.

music

Music is sound formed into pretty patterns. The Muppet Babies are making **music**.

Nn

nail

nails

You have **nails** on your fingers and toes.
A **nail** is also a small piece of metal with a round head on top.
Baby Skeeter hammers the **nail** into the board.

name

names

A **name** is a word for a person, place, or thing.

N, my **name** is Nancy, and my husband's **name** is Nick, and I come from Nebraska, and I sell nuts.

nap

naps

A **nap** is a short sleep that you take during the day.
Baby Animal takes his **nap** when he is sleepy.

near

Near is the opposite of far.
Baby Kermit is **near** the edge of this page.

neck

necks

Your **neck** is between your head and your shoulders.
Baby Bunsen wears a scarf around his **neck.**

nest

nests

A **nest** is the place where birds lay their eggs.
The bird sits in her **nest**.

new

New is the opposite of old.
Baby Piggy is showing off her **new** red shoes.

night

nights

Night is the opposite of day.
At **night**, the Muppet Babies sleep.

nine

Nine is the number after eight and before ten.
Can you count the **nine** nails in this picture?

no

No is the opposite of yes.
No, Baby Animal. Don't draw on this page!

nod

nods

A **nod** is when you move your head up and down. A **nod** usually means yes.
Simon says: **Nod** your head!

noise

noises

A **noise** is a loud sound. Baby Animal likes to make **noise** with pots and pans.

none

None means not any. Baby Skeeter has nine nails; Baby Gonzo has **none**.

noon

Noon is twelve o'clock in the middle of the day. **Noon** is a good time for lunch.

nose

noses

A **nose** is what people and animals smell with. Baby Gonzo's **nose** can almost touch his toes!

note

notes

A **note** is a short letter or message. Here is a **note** for you.

Dear reader,
Please go on to the next page.
Thank you.

nothing

Nothing means no thing.
This box has **nothing** in it.

now

Now means right this minute.
Baby Animal needs to wash
his hands right **now**.

number

numbers

A **number** tells you how many
of something you have.
The **number** of nuts near
the squirrel is nine.

nurse

nurses

A **nurse** is someone who
takes care of people in
school or in the hospital.
The **nurse** takes care
of Baby Beaker.

nut

nuts

A **nut** is a seed
with a hard shell.
The squirrel is saving
nuts for food in the winter.

O o

oar

oars

An **oar** is used to row a boat. This **boat** has two oars.

ocean

oceans

An **ocean** is the biggest body of water on earth. Fish swim in **oceans**.

off

Off is the opposite of on. The old man's hat falls **off** his head.

old

Old is the opposite of young. It is also the opposite of new. The **old** man lives in an **old** house.

on

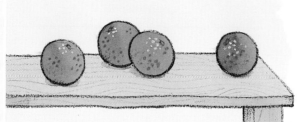

On is the opposite of off. There are four oranges **on** the table.

once

Once means at one time. **Once** there was an old woman who lived in a shoe.

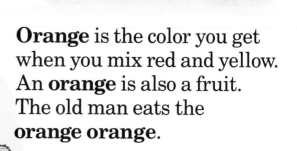

one

One is the number after zero and before two. The old man takes **one** orange off the table.

open

opens

You **open** something so that you or something else can get in or out of it. Baby Fozzie **opens** the door.

opposite

opposites

Two things that are completely different from each other are **opposites**. Up is the **opposite** of down.

orange

oranges

Orange is the color you get when you mix red and yellow. An **orange** is also a fruit. The old man eats the **orange orange**.

out

Out is the opposite of in.
Baby Fozzie goes **out** to play.

outside

Outside is the opposite of inside.
Baby Fozzie is **outside**.

oven

ovens

An **oven** is used
to bake food.
The Swedish Chef
bakes a pie
in the **oven**.

over

Over is the opposite of under.
The moon is **over** the cows.

Whoooo!

owl

owls

An **owl** is a bird with
big, round eyes that
sleeps all day.
Owls hoot at night.

P p

page

pages

A **page** is one of the pieces of paper in a book. Please look at each **page** in this book.

pail

pails

A **pail** is a container with a handle. Baby Piggy's **pail** is full of sand.

paint

paints

Paint is a colored liquid that you use to make pictures. Baby Gonzo uses pink **paint** to paint his picture.

pajamas

Pajamas are clothes to sleep in. Baby Fozzie puts on his **pajamas**.

pan

pans

A **pan** is a container
for cooking.
The Swedish Chef
cooks eggs in a **pan**.

pants

Pants are clothes that
cover your legs.
Baby Piggy wears
blue **pants**.

paper

papers

Paper is used for
writing, drawing, and
making books.
This page is made of **paper**.

park

parks

A **park** is a place with
plants, grass, and trees
that you can visit.
Baby Kermit plays
in the **park**.

part

parts

Parts are pieces of the whole.
The Muppet Babies ate
part of this birthday cake.

party

parties

A **party** is when people
get together to have fun.
Baby Piggy is having
a birthday **party**.

pea

peas

A **pea** is a green vegetable.
Pass the **peas**, please.

peach

peaches

A **peach** is a sweet,
round summer fruit.
The Swedish Chef picks
peaches for his pie.

pencil

pencils

A **pencil** is a tool for writing
and drawing.
Baby Fozzie draws
with a **pencil**.

people

People are men, women,
and children.
Many **people** live on earth.
You are one of them.

pet

pets

A **pet** is an animal
that lives with people.
Dogs and cats make
good **pets**.

piano

pianos

A **piano** is a musical instrument.
Baby Rowlf plays the **piano**.

picnic

picnics

A **picnic** is a party outside with food. The Muppet Babies are having a **picnic**.

picture

pictures

A **picture** shows you what someone or something looks like. Baby Gonzo paints a **picture** of a peach.

pie

pies

A **pie** is a baked food with a crust. It is sometimes filled with fruit. The Swedish Chef has baked two peach **pies**.

pig

pigs

A **pig** is an animal with short legs and a fat body. This **pig** lives on a farm.

pink

Pink is the color you get when you mix red and white. Baby Piggy wears a **pink** dress.

plant

plants

A **plant** is a living thing that is not an animal. Baby Kermit waters the **plants**.

Pp

plate
plates

A **plate** is a dish for food. Baby Gonzo has a lot of food on his **plate**.

play
plays

To **play** is to do something for fun. The Muppet Babies **play** leapfrog in the park.

please

Please is the word to use when you ask for something.

Please, Baby Piggy, may I have a peach?

pony
ponies

A **pony** is a small horse. Baby Scooter rides a **pony** in the park.

pool
pools

A **pool** is a small body of water. People swim in swimming **pools**.

pot
pots

A **pot** is a container for cooking. The Swedish Chef cooks noodles in a **pot**.

pretend

pretends

To **pretend** is to make believe.
Baby Skeeter **pretends**
that she's a cowgirl.

pull

pulls

To **pull** is to move something toward you.
Baby Gonzo **pulls** his red wagon.

puppy

puppies

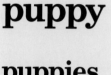

A **puppy** is a young dog.
The **puppy** sits in the red wagon.

purple

Purple is the color you get
when you mix red and blue.
These grapes are **purple**.

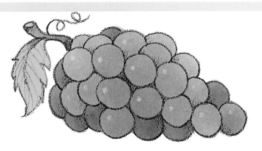

push

pushes

To **push** is to move
something away from you.
Baby Skeeter **pushes**
a toy truck.

put

puts

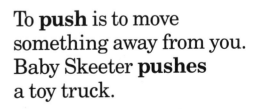

To **put** is to place
something somewhere.
Baby Skeeter **puts** the
toy truck in the chest.

Q q

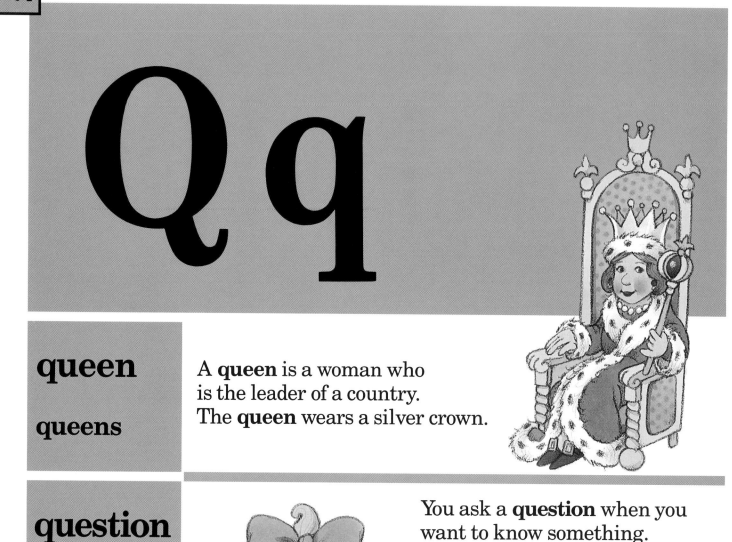

queen
queens

A **queen** is a woman who is the leader of a country. The **queen** wears a silver crown.

question
questions

You ask a **question** when you want to know something. This is a **question**:

What is your name?

quick

Quick means fast. **Quick**—ask Baby Piggy a question!

quiet

Quiet is when there is no noise. A library is a **quiet** place.

R r

rabbit
rabbits

A **rabbit** is a small, furry animal with long ears. **Rabbits** are sometimes called bunnies.

race
races

A **race** is a contest to see who is the fastest. The rabbit has won the **race.**

rain
rains

Rain is water that falls to the earth from the clouds. Baby Skeeter likes to play in the **rain.**

reach
reaches

To **reach** is to be able to touch something. Now Baby Animal can **reach** the toy truck.

read

reads

To **read** is to understand words on a page or a sign. Can you **read** this book?

rectangle

rectangles

A **rectangle** is a four-sided shape. Baby Rowlf draws a **rectangle.**

red

Red is a bright color. This fire truck is **red.**

ride

rides

To **ride** is to move in or on something. Baby Kermit **rides** on the train.

right

Right is the opposite of left. **Right** is also the opposite of wrong. The blue ball is on the **right.** That's **right!**

ring

rings

When you **ring** a bell, it makes a sound. Also, a **ring** is something you wear on your finger. This girl has **rings** on her fingers.

river
rivers

A **river** is a body of water that flows to the ocean.
Baby Gonzo sees the boats sail down the **river.**

road
roads

A **road** is a path for people, cars, and trucks.
This is the **road** to the barn.

rock
rocks

A **rock** is a big stone.
Baby Skeeter found
a pretty **rock** in the park.

rocket
rockets

A **rocket** travels
into outer space.
This **rocket** is going
to the stars.

roof
roofs

A **roof** is the cover
for a building.
The rain falls on the **roof.**

room
rooms

A **room** is inside
a building.
The kitchen is the **room**
where you cook dinner.

rose

roses

A **rose** is a flower that smells good. Baby Piggy has a red **rose.**

round

Round is the shape of a ball. The earth is also **round.**

row

rows

A **row** is a straight line of things.
Also, to **row** is to pull a boat through the water with oars. Baby Kermit **rows** the boat.

rug

rugs

A **rug** covers the floor. The big bear sits on the red **rug.**

ruler

rulers

A **ruler** is used to measure things. Baby Scooter measures the insect with a **ruler.**

run

runs

To **run** is to move your feet very fast. Baby Piggy **runs** down the road.

Ss

sad

Sad is the opposite of happy.
Baby Fozzie is **sad** because he has lost his teddy bear.

salt

Salt looks like white sand. We put **salt** on our food to make it taste good.
The water in the ocean has **salt** in it.

sand

Sand is tiny bits of rock you find on the beach.
Baby Fozzie's teddy bear is under the **sand.**

school

schools

School is a place where you learn and have fun, too.
Baby Kermit will learn to read in **school.**

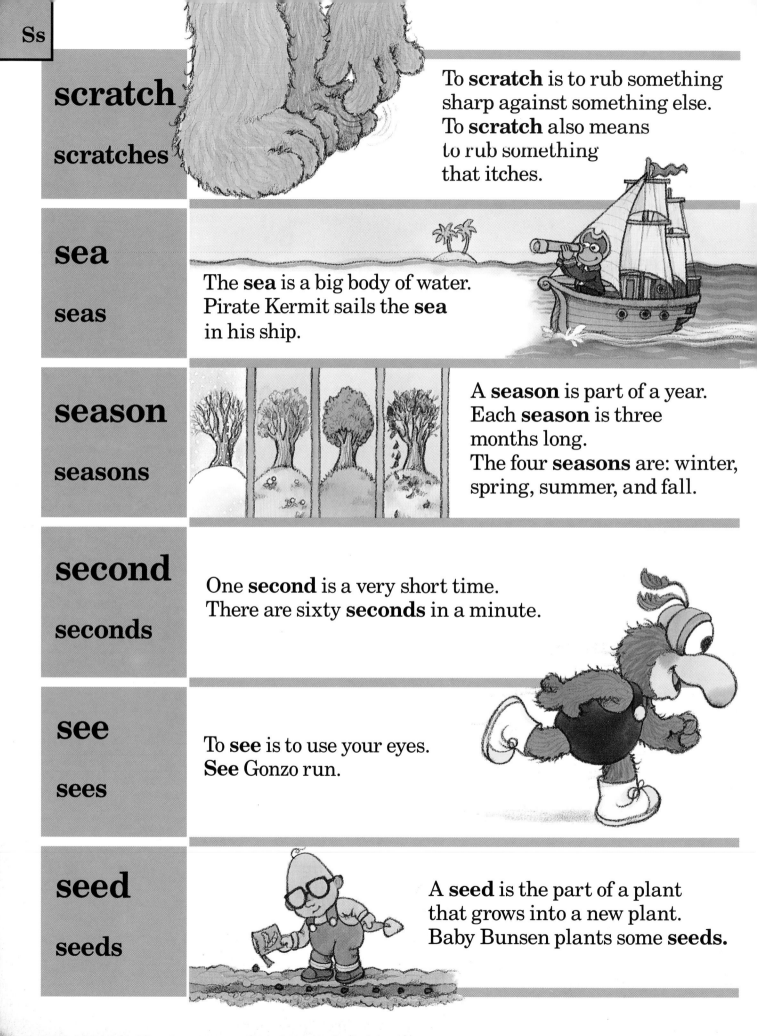

scratch

scratches

To **scratch** is to rub something sharp against something else. To **scratch** also means to rub something that itches.

sea

seas

The **sea** is a big body of water. Pirate Kermit sails the **sea** in his ship.

season

seasons

A **season** is part of a year. Each **season** is three months long. The four **seasons** are: winter, spring, summer, and fall.

second

seconds

One **second** is a very short time. There are sixty **seconds** in a minute.

see

sees

To **see** is to use your eyes. **See** Gonzo run.

seed

seeds

A **seed** is the part of a plant that grows into a new plant. Baby Bunsen plants some **seeds.**

seven

Seven is the number after six and before eight. Baby Bunsen has planted seven seeds.

shape

shapes

Shape is the outside form of something. There are many different shapes.

square

triangle

circle

diamond

heart

oval

rectangle

star

sheep

Sheep are gentle animals. A sheep's fur is called wool. Six sheep stand in the snow.

shell

shells

A shell is a hard covering. A turtle has a shell. So does an egg.

ship

ships

A ship is a big boat. Pirate Kermit's ship sails the seven seas.

shirt
shirts

Shirts are clothes that cover your chest and back.
Baby Fozzie puts on his **shirt.**

shoe
shoes

A **shoe** covers your foot. How many **shoes** can you wear at one time?

short

Short is the opposite of long. It is also the opposite of tall. Baby Kermit is too **short** to reach his book.

shoulder
shoulders

Your **shoulders** are between your neck and your arms. Simon says: Touch your **shoulders**!

sick

When you do not feel well, you are **sick**. When Baby Piggy is **sick**, the doctor takes care of her.

sign
signs

A **sign** tells you things in words or pictures. If you saw these **signs**, what would you do?

silver

Silver is a shiny metal. The queen's crown is made of **silver.**

sing
sings

To **sing** is to make music with your voice. Baby Rowlf **sings** and plays the piano.

sink
sinks

A **sink** is a bowl used for washing. Baby Piggy washes her hands at the **sink.**

sister
sisters

Your **sister** is a girl who has the same mother and father as you do. Skeeter is Scooter's **sister.**

sit
sits

To **sit** is to rest on your bottom. Simon says: **Sit** down on the chair.

six

Six is the number after five and before seven. There are **six** shoes on the rug.

skate

skates

To **skate** is to move with special shoes on your feet. The Muppet Babies **skate** down the road.

skin

skins

Skin is the outside covering on people and animals. Baby Kermit's **skin** is green.

skirt

skirts

A **skirt** is a piece of clothing that hangs down from the waist. Baby Skeeter wears a **skirt.**

sky

skies

The **sky** is above the earth. Baby Gonzo sees the birds fly in the blue **sky.**

sleep

sleeps

To **sleep** is to rest with your eyes closed. Baby Gonzo dreams about sheep when he **sleeps.**

slow

Slow is the opposite of fast. The turtle is a **slow** animal.

small

Small is the opposite of big.
The mouse is **small**;
the elephant is big.

smell
smells

You **smell** with your nose.
Baby Piggy **smells** the rose.

smile
smiles

You **smile** with your mouth
when you are happy.
Baby Kermit **smiles** at Piggy.

snake
snakes

A **snake** is a long, thin animal
with no arms or legs.
The **snake** lies in the sun.

sneeze
sneezes

To **sneeze** is to blow out air
suddenly through your
nose and mouth.
Baby Gonzo **sneezes.**

snow

Snow is white ice flakes
that fall from the sky.
Baby Kermit makes
a snowman out of **snow.**

Ss

soap

soaps

Soap is used to clean things. Baby Gonzo washes with **soap** and water.

sock

socks

A **sock** is a soft covering for the foot. Baby Scooter takes off his **sock.**

soft

Soft is the opposite of loud. **Soft** is also the opposite of hard. This pillow is **soft.**

son

sons

If you are a boy, you are the **son** of your mother and father. The **son** and daughter of the same mother and father are brother and sister.

sound

sounds

A **sound** is something you hear. Baby Fozzie hears the **sound** of the dinner bell.

soup

soups

Soup is a food made with water or milk. Some **soups** have vegetables in them.

spell
spells

To **spell** is to arrange letters to make words. How do you **spell** "spell"?

spider
spiders

A **spider** is small and has eight legs. **Spiders** use their webs to catch insects to eat.

spoon
spoons

A **spoon** is for eating and mixing. It is easy to eat soup with a **spoon.**

spring
springs

Spring is the season between winter and summer. Flowers grow in the **spring.**

square
squares

A **square** is a shape that has four sides that are the same length. Baby Kermit's book is a **square.**

squirrel
squirrels

A **squirrel** is a small animal that lives in trees and likes to eat nuts. This **squirrel** lives in the park.

stand

stands

To **stand** is to be up on your feet.
Simon says: **Stand** up.

star

stars

A **star** is a bright object far out in space.
At night, you can sometimes see the **stars.**

step

steps

Steps are stairs.
Also, to **step** is to move one foot.
Baby Rowlf **steps** over the stick.

stick

sticks

A **stick** is a long,
thin piece of wood.
Also, glue helps things
stick together.

stomach

stomachs

Your **stomach** is between
your waist and your legs.
Simon says: Put your hands
on your **stomach.**

stop

stops

Stop is the opposite of go.
Baby Kermit holds the
sign that says **stop.**

store
stores

A **store** is a place where you buy things. Baby Skeeter buys her shoes in a **store.**

story
stories

A **story** tells about something happening. Some **stories** are made up, but others are true. The father reads a **story** to his son.

street
streets

A **street** is a road in a city or town. There are stores on this **street.**

string
strings

String is thin cord or thread. **String** can tie things together or hold beads. Baby Kermit holds the **string** at the end of his kite.

sugar

Sugar makes food taste sweet. Brush your teeth after eating foods with **sugar.**

summer
summers

Summer is the season between spring and fall. The Muppet Babies go to the beach in the **summer.**

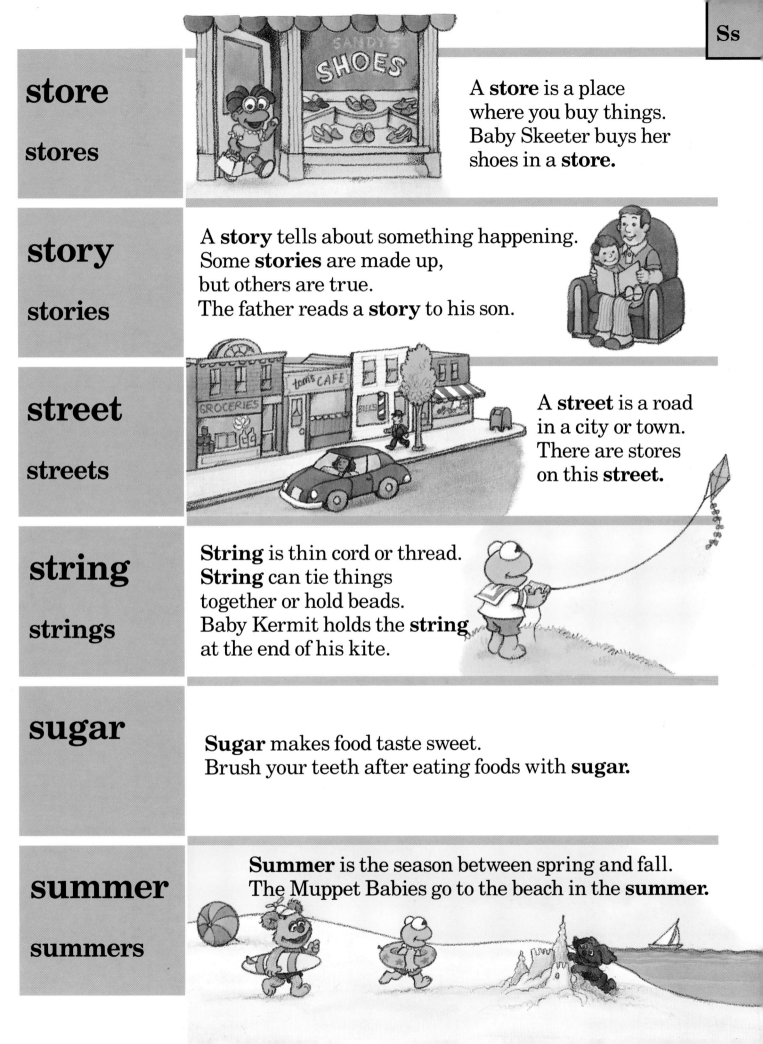

sun

The **sun** is a star. It gives the earth light and heat. The earth moves slowly around the **sun.**

swan

swans

A **swan** is a bird with a long neck. Most **swans** are white.

sweater

sweaters

A **sweater** covers the top part of your body and keeps you warm. Baby Scooter wears a blue **sweater.**

sweet

Sugar and honey make food taste **sweet.** Ice cream is a **sweet** dessert.

swim

swims

To **swim** is to move through the water. Frogs like to **swim.**

swing

swings

A **swing** is something you sit on that moves back and forth. Baby Piggy swings on a **swing** in the park.

Tt

table

tables

A **table** is furniture to eat at and work at. The Muppet Babies eat lunch at the **table.**

tail

tails

A **tail** is a part of an animal's body. The dog has a white **tail.**

take

takes

Take is the opposite of give. Baby Gonzo **takes** a carrot from Kermit.

talk

talks

Go bye-bye!

To **talk** is to say words. Baby Animal is learning to **talk.**

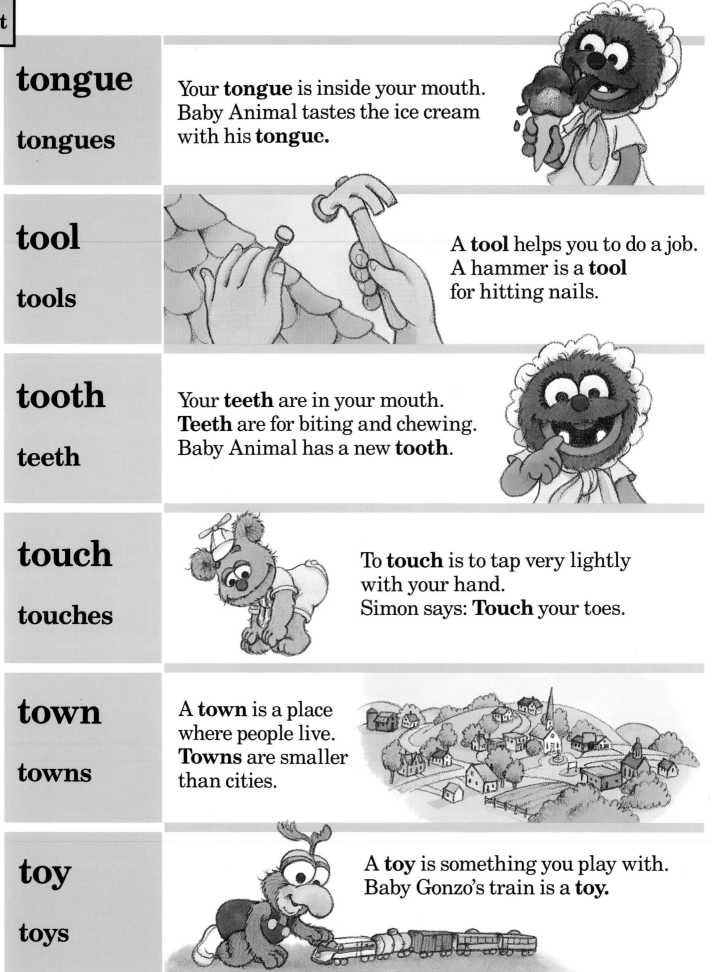

Tt

tongue

tongues

Your **tongue** is inside your mouth. Baby Animal tastes the ice cream with his **tonguc.**

tool

tools

A **tool** helps you to do a job. A hammer is a **tool** for hitting nails.

tooth

teeth

Your **teeth** are in your mouth. **Teeth** are for biting and chewing. Baby Animal has a new **tooth.**

touch

touches

To **touch** is to tap very lightly with your hand. Simon says: **Touch** your toes.

town

towns

A **town** is a place where people live. **Towns** are smaller than cities.

toy

toys

A **toy** is something you play with. Baby Gonzo's train is a **toy.**

train
trains

A **train** has wheels and an engine. You ride on a **train**. All aboard the **train**!

tree
trees

A **tree** is a large plant. Some **trees** lose their leaves in the fall.

triangle
triangles

A **triangle** is a shape with three sides. Baby Animal draws a **triangle.**

truck
trucks

A **truck** is a large car with wheels and an engine. This **truck** carries trees.

turtle
turtles

A **turtle** is an animal with a hard shell. The **turtles** swim in the water.

two

Two is the number after one and before three. Baby Piggy has **two** arms, **two** legs, **two** ears, and **two** eyes.

U u

umbrella
umbrellas

An **umbrella** keeps you dry in the rain. Baby Kermit holds an **umbrella.**

uncle
uncles

Your **uncle** is the brother of your mother or father. The child of your **uncle** and aunt is your cousin.

under

Under is the opposite of over. Baby Animal hides **under** the bed.

understand

understands

When you **understand** something, you know it or have a clear idea of it. Baby Kermit **understands** that two comes after one and before three.

undress

undresses

To **undress** means to take off your clothes.
Baby Animal **undresses** before he takes his bath.

unhappy

Unhappy means not happy.
Baby Animal is **unhappy** because he can't find his rubber duck.

up

Up is the opposite of down.
Baby Kermit goes **up** the stairs.

use

uses

To **use** is to put into action.
The man **uses** a hammer to build a doghouse.

Vv

vacation
vacations

A **vacation** is time away from work or school. Some people go to the beach on their **vacation.**

van
vans

A **van** is a kind of truck. When families move from one house to another house, they use a moving **van.**

vase
vases

A **vase** is a container for flowers. There are red roses in this **vase.**

vegetable
vegetables

A **vegetable** is a kind of food. Peas, carrots, and beans are all **vegetables.**

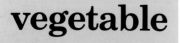

very

Very means more than or a lot. The van on the left is big, but the van on the right is **very** big.

view

views

A **view** is what you can see from somewhere. This window has a **view** of the ocean.

visit

visits

To **visit** is to go to see someone or someplace. The brother and sister **visit** their uncle.

voice

voices

Your **voice** is the sound that comes out of your mouth. You sing and talk with your **voice.**

vote

votes

To **vote** is to say if you like something or not. The Muppet Babies **vote** for their favorite game.

W w

wagon

wagons

A **wagon** has four wheels and is used to carry things. Baby Kermit pulls his blocks in the red **wagon.**

waist

waists

Your **waist** is between your chest and your stomach. Simon says: Put your hands on your **waist.**

walk

walks

To **walk** is to go by moving your feet forward. Baby Rowlf **walks** across the floor.

wall

walls

A **wall** is the side of a room or house. Baby Animal draws on the **wall.**

want

wants

To **want** something means you would like to have it. Baby Piggy **wants** a glass of water.

warm

Warm is between hot and cold. Baby Fozzie is **warm** under his blanket.

wash

washes

To **wash** is to make something clean. Baby Animal **washes** the wall.

water

Water is a clear liquid. Lakes, rivers, oceans, and rain are made of water. Plants, animals, and people need **water** to live.

wave

waves

When water goes up and down, it is called a **wave.** To **wave** is also to move your hand. Baby Gonzo **waves** good-bye.

wear

wears

To **wear** is to put something on. You can **wear** a sweater or a smile.

week
weeks

A **week** is seven days.
They are: Sunday, Monday,
Tuesday, Wednesday, Thursday,
Friday, and Saturday.

well

A **well** is a big hole with
water at the bottom.
Also, **well** is the opposite of sick.
Baby Kermit felt sick this
morning, but now he feels **well.**

wet

Wet is the opposite of dry.
Water is **wet.**

whale
whales

A **whale** is a big animal that lives in the ocean.
Pirate Kermit sees **whales** from his boat.

what

What is a word that often
asks a question.
What is that big animal
swimming in the water?

wheel
wheels

A **wheel** is something round
that helps make things move.
Trains, bicycles, tricyles, and
wagons have **wheels.**

when

When is a word that tells something about time. We will go outside **when** it stops raining.

where

Where is a word that tells something about place. **Where** does the butterfly go when it rains?

white

White is when there is no color at all. The **white** bear walks in the **white** snow.

who

Who is a word for a person. **Who** is wearing the mask?

whole

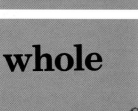

The **whole** is all of something. Baby Animal ate the **whole** pie.

why

Why is a word that asks for what reason. **Why** is Baby Gonzo wearing a mask?

wild

Wild animals don't usually live with people. This lion is **wild.**

wind

winds

Wind is air that moves. The **wind** blows the leaves off the trees.

window

windows

A **window** is an opening covered with glass. This house has five **windows.**

wing

wings

Birds, bats, and insects use **wings** to fly. Airplanes have **wings,** too.

winter

winters

Winter is the season between fall and spring. In many places, it is cold in the **winter.**

wish

wishes

To **wish** for something is to want it very much. Baby Piggy **wishes** for a sunny day.

woman
women

When a girl grows up, she is a **woman.**
These **women** were once little girls.

wood

Wood comes from trees.
Some people build houses
out of **wood.**

word
words

A **word** is made of letters and has a meaning.
You are reading **words** right now.

work
works

To **work** is to do something
that has to be done.
People often **work** to make
money to live.

write
writes

To **write** is to put words on paper.
Baby Piggy **writes** a letter
to Baby Kermit.

wrong

Wrong is the opposite of right.
This is the **wrong** answer.

X x Y y

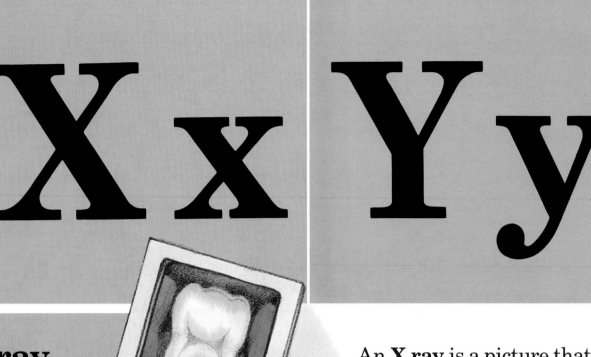

X ray
X rays

An **X ray** is a picture that shows the inside of something. This is an **X ray** of a tooth.

xylophone
xylophones

A **xylophone** is a musical instrument that you hit to make sounds. Baby Rowlf plays the **xylophone.**

yard
yards

A **yard** is the ground around a house. Baby Piggy grows flowers in her **yard.**

yawn
yawns

When you are sleepy, you open your mouth to **yawn.** Baby Animal **yawns** before his nap.

year

years

A **year** is a long time. There are twelve months in a **year.** Your birthday comes once every **year.**

yellow

Yellow is the color of the sun. Baby Piggy has some **yellow** flowers.

yes

Yes is the opposite of no.

Yes, Baby Piggy. I would like some flowers.

yesterday

Yesterday is the day before today. Was **yesterday** a rainy day or a sunny day?

young

Young is the opposite of old. A child is a **young** person.

yo-yo

yo-yos

A **yo-yo** is a toy that goes up and down on a string. The child plays with a **yo-yo.**

Z z

zebra

zebras

A **zebra** is a black-and-white animal with four legs. A **zebra** looks like a horse with pajamas on.

zero

Zero means none or nothing. **Zero** comes before one. If you have **zero** zebras, you have no zebras.

zipper

zippers

A **zipper** is used to open and close things. Baby Gonzo zips his **zipper**.

zoo

zoos

A **zoo** is a place where people come to see wild animals. The Muppet Babies visit the zebras at the **zoo**.